#4

Coach Hyatt Is a Riot!

Dan Gutman

Pictures by
Jim Paillot

HarperTrophy®
An Imprint of HarperCollinsPublishers

For Emma

Harper Trophy® is a registered trademark of HarperCollins Publishers.

Coach Hyatt Is a Riot!

Text copyright © 2009 by Dan Gutman

Illustrations copyright © 2009 by Jim Paillot

All rights reserved. Printed in the United States of America.

No part of this book may be used or reproduced in any manner whatsoever without written permission except in the case of brief quotations embodied in critical articles and reviews. For information address HarperCollins Children's Books, a division of HarperCollins Publishers, 195 Broadway, New York, NY 10007.

www.harpercollinschildrens.com

Library of Congress Cataloging-in-Publication Data

Gutman, Dan.

   Coach Hyatt is a riot! / Dan Gutman ; pictures by Jim Paillot. — 1st ed.

     p.   cm. — (My weird school daze ; #4)

   Summary: A new football coach arrives at school and, with help from an unexpected new team member, the Moose win a game.

   ISBN 978-0-06-155408-7 (lib. bdg.) — ISBN 978-0-06-155406-3 (pbk.)

   [1. Football–Fiction. 2. Schools–Fiction. 3. Coaches (Athletics–Fiction. 4. Humorous stories.] I. Paillot, Jim, ill. II. Title.

PZ7.G9846Co 2009   2008031421

[Fic]–dc22   CIP

                                                               AC

Typography by Joel Tippie

First Edition

18 19 20   BRR   40 39 38 37 36 35 34 33 32

Contents

1 The Thing I Love   1

2 Coach Hyatt Is Mean   9

3 Cheerleaders Who Throw Up   16

4 Weird Training Methods   24

5 Dancing in the End Zone   31

6 Rufus the Doofus   42

7 The Sharks   50

8 The First Half   58

9 Halftime   66

10 Our Secret Weapon   74

11 The Moose Goes Nuts   79

12 The Secret Play   88

13 UFM*   97

The Thing
I Love

My name is A.J. and I *love* school.

Going to school is just *so* much fun! I wish we could go to school at night. I wish we could go to school on the weekend. I wish we never had vacations.

Just kidding!

I *hate* school! Do you know what I would rather do than go to school? I would rather eat a dead-bug sandwich. No, I would rather eat a *live*-bug sandwich. That would be even worse than a dead-bug sandwich, because the bugs would still be moving around in the sandwich while I was eating it. Ugh, disgusting! But even more disgusting than eating a live-bug sandwich is going to school.

I don't hate *everything*, you know. Some stuff I love. Like video games. And skateboarding. And trick biking.

I'll tell you the one thing that I *really* love more than anything in the world. And it's *not* Andrea Young, this annoying girl in my class with curly brown hair.

I love Pee Wee Football.

In the fall I play football every Saturday. Football is cool because you get to push and shove and yell and knock kids on their butts. And the best part is, you don't even get punished!

At school, if you push and shove and yell and knock kids on their butts, you have to go to the principal's office. But in football you're *supposed* to push and shove and yell and knock kids on their butts.

That's why I hate school and love Pee Wee Football. If you ask me, the world would be a better place if they closed all the schools and turned them into Pee Wee Football camps.

The only problem is, my team *stinks*!

We're called the Moose,* and we lost every game last season. Every game!

The good news is, we're getting a new coach this year named Coach Hyatt. I bet he'll be a lot better than our old coach, Mr. Boozer. Mr. Boozer was a loser.

I put on my uniform and shoulder pads to get ready for our first practice. Shoulder pads are cool because they make it look like you have big muscles. Our uniform is red, and we have red helmets with a lightning bolt down the middle.

Mom drove me to practice at the high school field. We got out of the car and

---

* One goose and another goose are geese. But one moose and another moose aren't meese. Nobody knows why.

4

looked around until we found the other guys in the seventy-pound league.

"Give me a good-bye hug, A.J.," my mom said.

Mom is always trying to hug me, especially in front of other kids. Moms are weird.

"Not now, Mom."

"Hug me, A.J.," my mom said.

"No way."

"I want a hug, A.J.," my mom said.

"I don't *think* so."

Mom reached out to grab me. But I faked left. Then I faked right. Then I faked left again. Ha-ha! I totally faked out my mom! She can't play football to save her life. Eat my dust, Mom!

There were around twenty kids with red uniforms like mine. Some of them were in my class, and some others I didn't know.

"I can't wait to meet Coach Hyatt," said my friend Michael, who never ties his shoes.

"I hope he lets me be the kicker," said Ryan, who will eat anything, even stuff that isn't food.

"I hope he lets me play fullback," said Neil, who we call the nude kid even though he wears clothes.

"I hope he lets me be the quarterback because—"*

I didn't get the chance to finish my sentence, because that's when a cool car pulled up. It looked just like a real car, only smaller. Michael knows all about cars. He said it was a Mini Cooper.

Coach Hyatt and some kid got out of the little car. They were coming over to us. The coach had on a red shirt and a red

---

* It's called a quarterback because in ancient times a football cost seventy-five cents. When primitive people used a dollar to buy one, they got a quarter back.

hat, and wore a whistle around his neck.

But there was something really strange about him.

He wasn't a him at all!

Coach Hyatt was . . . a *lady*!

Coach Hyatt Is Mean

Girls aren't supposed to be football coaches! That's a scientific fact. What do girls know about pushing and shoving and knocking kids on their butts? Girls only care about puppies and butterflies, and what color nail polish they have on.

But the lady who got out of the Mini

Cooper *was* Coach Hyatt. I knew because she had a big name tag on her shirt that said MY NAME IS COACH HYATT. She blew her whistle.

"Line up!" Coach Hyatt barked.

We all looked at her. I wasn't about to line up for some lady coach. Ladies don't know the first thing about football. My mom thinks that sacking the quarterback means you put a bag over his head.

Like I said, moms are weird.

Coach Hyatt blew her whistle again.

"I SAID, 'LINE UP!'"

We all lined up. Coach Hyatt looked mean. We were all shaking and shivering and quivering.

"Now listen up!"
she barked. "This is my
son, Wyatt. He's on the team, whether

you like it or not."

Wyatt Hyatt? I knew right away this kid was weird.

Wyatt was a little guy. He looked like he was in first grade. Wyatt was picking his nose and wiping it on his helmet.

"I hope you kids are ready to *work*!" barked Coach Hyatt.

"Uh, we're here to play football," I told her.

"Well, you're gonna work! And you're gonna sweat! And you're gonna stink! And you know what?"

"What?" we all asked.

"You're gonna *like* it!" she barked.

Coach Hyatt was scary! Some kids were

already whimpering and saying they wanted to go home.

"Aren't you taking this a little too seriously?" asked Michael. "We're only eight years old."

"When I was eight," Coach Hyatt told us, "I built a log cabin with my bare hands."

I didn't know what that had to do with anything. But I wasn't about to complain, because Coach Hyatt seemed so mean.

"Can I go to the bathroom?" one kid asked.

"No!" Coach Hyatt barked. "Bathrooms are for losers. You're weak! I'll chew you up and spit you out. I'm gonna turn you ragamuffins into winners!"

I didn't know
what a ragamuffin
was. I figured it must
be a muffin made out of
rags, or a rag made out of
muffins. But it didn't matter.
If winners are people who
aren't allowed to go to the
bathroom, I think I'd rather
be a loser.

I didn't even have to
go to the bathroom; but
after Coach Hyatt said
we weren't allowed to,
suddenly I had to. I hate
when that happens.

She made us run all the way around the field, which is like a million hundred miles. Then she made us run all the way around the field *backward*, which is even farther. Then she made us run all the way around the field sideways!

We were huffing and puffing and holding our sides. When we finished, Wyatt picked his nose. There was a big jug of Gatorade on the bench, but Coach Hyatt wouldn't let us drink any.

"Can we take a break now?" Ryan asked.

"No!" Coach Hyatt barked. "Breaks are for losers."

I thought I was gonna die.

Cheerleaders
Who Throw Up

When my mom dropped me off for our next practice, she didn't even *try* to hug me. Some of the ragamuffins from the first practice didn't come back. I guess they couldn't take it.

Coach Hyatt wasn't there yet. But you'll never believe in a million hundred years who pulled up in a blue minivan.

A bunch of *girls*!

It was that annoying Andrea Young, her crybaby friend Emily, and some other girly girls. They piled out of the minivan and came over to us.

"Hi, Arlo!" said Andrea, who calls me by my real name because she knows I don't like it. Andrea was wearing earrings that were little footballs and a necklace shaped like a goalpost.

"What are YOU doing here?" I asked.

"We're cheerleaders!" said Emily.

I knew Andrea took ballet classes after school. She takes Irish step dancing, too. And modern dance. And clog dancing.*

---

* Clog dancing is a dance that plumbers do to make water go down the drain.

17

That girl sure likes to dance. But I didn't know she did cheerleading, too.

"Since when do you do cheerleading?" I asked Andrea.

"I've been cheering since I was four years old," Andrea said.

"Don't you get tired?" I asked.

"Very funny, Arlo."

"How can you cheer for football?" Michael asked Andrea. "You probably don't even know what a touchdown is."

"Yeah!" agreed Ryan.

"A touchdown is a scoring play in which any part of the ball, while legally in the possession of a player who is inbounds, crosses the plane of the opponent's goal line," Andrea said. "I read a book about football, so now I know all about it."

I hate her. Why can't a goalpost fall on Andrea's head?

"Do you want to hear one of our cheers?" asked Emily. "We wrote them ourselves."

"Oh yes," I said, "I'd love to . . . in the next century."

So of course Andrea and Emily did their

cheer anyway. They danced around while chanting:

"Jump in the air! Fall in the dirt.
Just make sure no one gets hurt!
Go . . . Moose!"

"That cheer is lame," I told them.

"You're mean, Arlo!" Andrea said.

Their cheer *was* lame. Football cheers should be cool. I made up a cheer on the spot that was way better than their dumb cheer.

"Bust 'em! Beat 'em! Make 'em bleed!
Hit 'em till their eyeballs fall out."

"That doesn't even rhyme," Emily said.

"And it's so violent!" said Andrea. "We only do positive cheers that don't hurt anyone's feelings."

"Yes," said Emily. "It's not whether you win or lose; it's how you play the game. Isn't the important thing to have fun?"

"No!" I said. "Where'd you get that crazy idea?"

The girls did one of their routines where they throw each other up in the air while they do a cheer.

"Laugh and play and shout and sing!
Winning isn't everything!
Go . . . Moose!"

What a lame cheer. But I had to admit that Andrea and her friends were pretty good at throwing each other up. In the air, that is. If you threw up a person, it would be disgusting.

I remembered that in fizz ed, Andrea is always the one who can balance feathers, juggle scarves, and do stuff better than anybody else. She's a good soccer player, too. But she's still annoying.

"Do you want to see us make a human pyramid?" asked Emily.

"Why don't you go to Egypt and make a *real* pyramid," I suggested. "And don't come back."

"Humphf!" said Andrea. She and the

other cheerleaders stormed away to practice at the other end of the field.

When girls get mad, they always say "Humphf." Nobody knows why.

Weird Training Methods

Coach Hyatt pulled up in her Mini Cooper with her weird son, Wyatt Hyatt. She blew her whistle.

"Line up!" she barked. "I hope you raga-muffins are ready to work today."

"Are we gonna run more laps?" Michael asked.

"No!"

"Are we gonna do jumping jacks?" asked Ryan.

"No!"

"Are we gonna do push-ups?" asked Neil the nude kid.

"No!"

"Sit-ups?" I asked. "Touch our toes?"

"No!"

"Then what are we gonna do?" Michael asked.

"You're going to pick up my car," said Coach Hyatt.

"WHAT?!"

"You heard me! Pick up my car!"

"I can't pick up a car," I said.

"You can't pick up a car by *yourself*," said Coach Hyatt. "But I bet that all of you can pick up my car *together*."

She told half of the team to grab the front bumper of the Mini Cooper and the other half of the team to grab the back bumper. Wyatt just picked his nose.

"Okay," Coach Hyatt said, "when I blow my whistle, pick up the car."

She blew her whistle, and we pulled up with all our might. And you'll never believe in a million hundred years what happened.

We picked up the Mini Cooper!

"WOW," we all said, which is "MOM" upside down.

"Look at that!" Coach Hyatt barked. "You ragamuffins picked up a *car*! That's teamwork! My motto is, 'If you can pick up a car, you'll go far.'"

It seemed to me that you could go a lot

farther if you got *in* the car and drove it somewhere. But still, it was cool to pick up a car, even if it was a Mini Cooper.

Coach Hyatt had us pair off and pass the football back and forth. She said she wanted to see who could throw the ball and catch it. Ryan got teamed up with Neil. I got teamed up with Michael. Wyatt just picked his nose.

I'm a good quarterback. Michael and I were passing and catching pretty good

when one of my throws got past him. The ball rolled all the way over near the cheer-leaders. Andrea picked it up.

"Hey, throw it back!" Michael yelled.

"What's the magic word?" Andrea asked.

"Please?" said Michael.

Andrea picked up the football. And you'll never believe in a million hundred years what happened next.

She threw it *way* over all our heads!

I mean, it must have gone fifty yards in the air. And it was a perfect spiral, too.

"WOW!" we all said, which is "MOM" upside down.

Dancing in the End Zone

When we arrived for our next practice, Andrea and the girly cheerleaders were practicing their routines at the other end of the field.

"Losing! Winning! We won't lie!
We're most happy with a tie!
Go . . . Moose!"

What a lame cheer. Finally, Coach Hyatt showed up in her Mini Cooper with her nose-picking son, Wyatt Hyatt. There was a guy sitting in the car with them, but he didn't get out. Hmm, that was weird. Coach Hyatt blew her whistle.

"Line up!"

"Are we gonna pick up your car again today?" asked Neil.

"No!" the coach barked. "Today you ragamuffins are going to learn the most important part of football—how to do an end zone dance."

"A what?" asked Ryan.

"After you score a touchdown, you have

to do a dance in the end zone," Coach Hyatt said.

Then Coach Hyatt showed us her end zone dance. She shook her butt, lifted a leg over her head, hopped up and down for a while, and then put her hands in the air and waved them around like a crazy person.

Coach Hyatt is a riot!

"Now you try," she told us.

We all shook our butts, lifted one of our legs over our heads, hopped up and down for a while, and put our hands in the air and waved them around like crazy people. Wyatt just picked his nose.

"Can we have some Gatorade now?" asked Ryan.

"No!" barked Coach Hyatt.

After we learned the end zone dance, the coach went to her car. Remember that guy who was sitting in it? Well, it turned out he wasn't a guy at all. He wasn't a girl, either.

He was a dummy.

"This is my friend Elvis," Coach Hyatt said as she carried the dummy over to us.

Sure enough, the dummy looked just like the real Elvis. It sounded like him too. Coach Hyatt pushed a button on the back of the dummy and it started singing, "You ain't nothin' but a hound dog. . . ."

Coach Hyatt said we were going to use Elvis to practice our tackling. Tackling is fun, because you get to knock the dummy on its butt.

We all lined up to tackle Elvis. I got to go first because my name begins with *A*.

"Okay, A.J.," said Coach Hyatt. "I want

you to pretend this is somebody you really hate."

That was easy.

"I'm gonna pretend it's Andrea!" I told the guys.

"You ain't nothin' but a hound dog!" sang Elvis.

I pretended that the Elvis dummy was Andrea and rammed it as hard as I could.

"Don't be cruel!" sang Elvis as I got off him. "Oooooooooh! I'm all shook up."

"Good job, A.J.!" said Coach Hyatt.

Each of us got to tackle the Elvis dummy five times. It was cool. Coach Hyatt showed us how to go for the legs so the runner would fall down. Wyatt just picked his nose. Doesn't that kid ever run out of boogers?

When we were finished, the coach blew her whistle and said we could take a drink from the Gatorade jug.

That's when Little Miss Perfect came over. She had on a cheerleading uniform and was holding pom-poms in her hands.

"That was a very violent exercise you were doing," Andrea told us. "Is it really necessary to hit the dummy so hard? I think that leads to violent behavior in children."

"Can you possibly be more boring?" I asked Andrea. "Why don't you go back to *your* side of the field and work on your lame cheers?"

"Humphf!" said Andrea. Then she stormed off to do more lame cheers with her friends.

"We don't hate and we don't boo!
We respect the other team, too!
Go . . . Moose!"

After everybody had some Gatorade, Coach Hyatt taught us how to punt the ball. Punting is hard. I punted the ball really far, but I couldn't make it go straight. One of my punts landed over near the cheerleaders. Andrea picked it up.

I remembered the last time she got her

hands on the ball. She threw it over our heads.

"Don't throw it," I told Andrea. "Just *bring* it back."

"What's the magic word, Arlo?" asked Andrea.

"Now!" I yelled.

"Well, okay," Andrea said, "but you're going to have to tackle me for it."

Me and the guys laughed.

A *cheerleader* thought she could run past a bunch of trained football players! Ha!

"I'd like to see you try!" I yelled.

Andrea started running toward us.

"Get her!" I yelled.

Andrea faked out Michael.

Then she faked out Ryan.

Then she faked out Neil.

Andrea was faking out *everybody*! She was running down the field, and nobody could stop her!

Nobody but *me*, that is. After she faked everybody else out, I was the only player between Andrea and the goal line.

"You're not getting past me," I told her.

"Oh yes, I am, Arlo."

"Oh no, you're not," I told Andrea.

We went back and forth like that for a while. Then Andrea faked left.

Then she faked right.

Then she faked left again.

But I wasn't gonna fall for her lame fakes. I grabbed her legs and slammed her to the ground. All the guys cheered.

"Oooooh!" Ryan said. "A.J. tackled Andrea. They must be in *love*!"

"When are you gonna get married?" asked Michael.

If those guys weren't my best friends, I would hate them.

41

Rufus
the Doofus

Coach Hyatt showed up at our next practice with Wyatt the Nose Picker. A big, brown, rubber thing was strapped to the roof of the Mini Cooper.

"What's that big, brown, rubber thing?" we all asked.

"Last time I told you ragamuffins about

the end zone dance," the coach said. "Today I want to talk about another very important part of football—the blimp."

"You got a *blimp*?" asked Ryan.

We all got excited, because blimps are cool.

"Not exactly," Coach Hyatt said as she took the big, brown, rubber thing off the roof of her car and put it on the grass. "I couldn't get a blimp. But I got something even *better*!"

"What is it?" Michael asked.

"Oh, you'll see," said Coach Hyatt.

She attached a bike pump to the big, brown, rubber thing and started pumping air into it. It got bigger and bigger. And you'll never believe in a million hundred years what it turned out to be.

It was a giant, inflatable moose!

"This is Rufus," said Coach Hyatt. "He's our mascot. I call him Rufus T. Moose. The *T* stands for 'the.' Rufus the Moose will float over the field and inspire us to victory."

"Where'd you get him?" I asked, "Rent-A-Moose?"

"No, Rent-A-Blimp," Coach Hyatt said. "Some other team got the last blimp, so I was able to get a discount on Rufus. Isn't he awesome?"

No, he wasn't. Rufus the Moose was kind of wrinkled, and one of his antlers looked like it was about to fall off.

Rufus the Doofus was more like it.

I didn't tell Coach Hyatt that her moose was lame because I didn't want to hurt her feelings.

The coach tied Rufus the Doofus to a tree so he wouldn't blow away. Then she wheeled a big whiteboard out of the equipment shed. It was like the whiteboards we use at school.

"It's time to go over some plays," Coach Hyatt told us.

She drew a bunch of Xs and Os on the board to represent the players on our team and another team. Then she drew lines to show where each of us was supposed to run. We went over a bunch of running plays and passing plays. I knew most of them already from last season.

"And now," the coach said as she looked around to make sure nobody was watching, "I'm going to show you our *Secret* Play."

Oooooh! We all leaned forward. Secret plays are cool because, well, anything involving secrets is cool.

Coach Hyatt began drawing lines all over the board.

"A.J., you're the quarterback, so you go here," she barked. "Ryan, you go here. Michael, you go here. Neil, you go here. Wyatt, you go here. Wyatt will hike the ball to A.J. A.J. will flip it to Ryan. Ryan will pass it to Michael. Michael will lateral it to Neil. Neil will hand it off to Wyatt. Wyatt will run it into the end zone for a touchdown. Got it?"

"Got it!" we all shouted, even though none of us got it. Coach Hyatt's Secret

Play made no sense at all, but none of us wanted to look dumb.

"Okay, let's try it," said Coach Hyatt.

We all got into position.

"Hut-one!"* I shouted. "Hut-two! HIKE!"

And we all ran into each other.

It was a big mess of kids in a gigantic pile. There were arms and legs flailing around. It looked like one of those tanks full of lobsters you see in the supermarket. Unfortunately, I was the lobster on the bottom.

"Owwww, my leg!" I yelled.

---

* Quarterbacks always say "Hut" before the ball is hiked. That's because in ancient times the first primitive football players lived in huts.

"Walk it off, A.J.!" Coach Hyatt barked when the last kid climbed off me.

"I think my leg might be broken," I said.

"Broken?" barked the coach. "When I was your age, if my leg was broken, I would go out and build a log cabin with my bare hands."

What did that have to do with anything?

I thought I was gonna die.

The Sharks

Luckily, my leg wasn't broken after all. It was just a little sore. We practiced really hard that week until we knew all the plays. Finally, it was time for our first game. We were playing a team called the Sharks.

It was a beautiful Saturday. When we

came out of the locker room, there was Rufus the Doofus floating over the field. And you'll never believe in a million hundred years what was floating in the air right next to Rufus.

A blimp!

And you know what it said on the side of the blimp? GO SHARKS!

How come the Sharks got a blimp and we got a lame, inflatable moose? It totally wasn't fair!

Andrea and the other cheerleaders were on the sideline with their pom-poms.

"Football has a kicker. Baseball has
a batter!

Whatever game we play, the score
  doesn't matter!
Go . . . Moose!"

What a lame cheer.

The bleachers were filled with parents and their cameras. A few moms were selling cookies. Some of the teachers from our school were there, too—Miss Holly, Mr. Macky, Ms. Coco, Ms. Hannah, Mr. Loring. I spotted my teacher, Mr. Granite. He comes from another planet called Etinarg. Me and the guys ran over to say hello to him.

"Do they have football on Etinarg?" asked Michael.

"Oh no," Mr. Granite said. "We play a

game called llabtoof."

"How do you play *that*?" Neil asked.

"It's very simple," Mr. Granite told us.
"There are thirteen glorps on each darge,

and they toss a pinker back and forth to see who can score the most floobs. The winner gets to urgle a flange."

That game sounded weird. I wanted to ask Mr. Granite more about llabtoof, but that's when the Sharks came out of their locker room. They had blue uniforms. We all stared as they jogged on to the field.

"Wow!" Ryan said. "Those guys are *huge*!"

He was right. The Sharks didn't look like they were humans. Their arms were bigger than my legs. Even their muscles had muscles.

"No way those guys weigh seventy pounds," said Michael.

"They look like they're in seventh grade," said Neil the nude kid.

"We can't beat *them*," said Ryan. "They're gonna kill us!"

"Can't we just pick up their car and carry it away?" I suggested.

"They came in a *bus*, dumbhead," said Ryan.

"They're awfully big, Coach," Michael said.

"The bigger they come, the harder they fall," Coach Hyatt told us.

"Yeah, but they're gonna fall on *us*," I said, "and we're gonna *die*!"

Wyatt just picked his nose. I'll tell you, that kid must have an unlimited supply of boogers.

Andrea and the other cheerleaders made one of their lame cheers:

"Winning! Losing! It depends!
Why can't we just all be friends?
Go . . . Moose!"

When the Sharks came out, their cheerleaders on the other side of the field started doing a cheer of their own. It didn't rhyme or anything, but it sounded a lot better than our cheers:

"Kill! Kill! Kill!
Crush the Moose!

Stomp them! Rip their faces off!

Remove their internal organs!"

"My life is over," I told the guys.

The First Half

It was time for the coin toss to decide which team would kick off. Me and Ryan are captains of the Moose, so we ran out to the middle of the field. So did two of the Sharks. The ref told us to shake hands.

One of the Sharks grabbed my hand. He didn't just shake it like a normal person.

He started squeezing. So I squeezed back. And he squeezed harder. And it really hurt! I thought I was gonna die. But just before my fingers were crushed, the Shark let go.

"Grrrrrr!" he said. "I eat shrimps like you for breakfast."

"So is your face," I replied, because I couldn't think of anything else to say.

The ref tossed the coin up and I called heads.

"Tails!" yelled the ref.

Bummer in the summer! We had to kick off.

Our team got into position. Ryan put the ball on the tee. All the grown-ups in the bleachers started cheering. The ref blew his whistle, and Ryan kicked off.

It was a pretty good kick, too. We all ran down the field to tackle the Shark who picked up the ball. The only problem was, there were giant Sharks running all over the place!

One of them knocked Michael on his butt.

One of them knocked Ryan on his butt.

One of them knocked *me* on my butt.

They were knocking all of us on our butts!*

"Run for your life!" Neil shouted.

_____

* Grown-ups get mad when you say "butt." Nobody knows why.

When I looked up from the ground, the Sharks were in the end zone dancing and high-fiving each other.

Sharks 6, Moose 0.

"That's all right! That's okay!
We're gonna win it anyway!
Go . . . Moose!"

The Sharks made the extra point and kicked off to us. Michael picked up the ball. But before he could take a step, he was knocked on his butt by some giant Shark. Michael fumbled the ball, and the next thing we knew, the Sharks were dancing and high-fiving each other again in the end zone.

Sharks 13, Moose 0.

"That's all right! That's okay!
We're gonna win next Saturday!
Go . . . Moose!"

You don't need to hear all the gory details of what happened in the first half. But whenever the Sharks had the ball, they ran right over us like we were made out of tissue paper and knocked us on our butts. Whenever we had the ball, they knocked us on our butts and took the ball away. It wasn't a pretty sight.

"It's okay that we're not great,
At least we all participate!
Go . . . Moose!"

What a lame cheer. Andrea and her friends were no help at all. The cheerleaders weren't looking very cheery.

Wyatt was useless. All he ever did was stand around and pick his nose.

And having Rufus the Doofus floating over the field wasn't doing us any good either.

Finally, the clock ran out. It was halftime. We had played two quarters, but it felt like a million. Our team was staggering all over the field. I was still on my hands and knees in the dirt after the last Shark touchdown.

"Hey, loser!" one of the Sharks said to me on his way to the locker room. "Where'd you get that lame moose?"

"Rent-A-Blimp," I told him.

The score at halftime: Sharks 77, Moose 0.

Halftime

9

We all trudged into the locker room like zombies. We were tired. Sore. Dirty. Depressed. It looked more like a hospital than a locker room. Wyatt Hyatt was lying on the floor picking his nose.

"I think I'm gonna die," I announced as I plopped down on a bench.

"Can we go home now?" asked Neil the nude kid.

Coach Hyatt blew her whistle.

"Okay," she barked. "Listen up! All you ragamuffins gather around and take a knee."

"Take a knee?" I asked. "Why should I take a knee?"

"Where do I get a knee to take?" asked Ryan. "And where should I take it?"

"What if somebody is using their knee and can't loan it to me?" asked Michael.

"I can't take my own knee," said Neil. "I need it. Whose knee should I take?"

"Just kneel down, boys," said Coach Hyatt.

"Oh."

"We're only behind by seventy-seven points," the coach told us. "There's still a lot of football to be played. Plenty of time to catch up."

Everybody groaned

"Can't we just forfeit the game, Coach?" I asked.

"Forfeit?" Coach Hyatt barked. "When I was your age and my team was behind by seventy-seven points, do you know what I would do?"

"What?" we all asked.

"I'd build a log cabin with my bare hands."

"Why would you do that?" asked Ryan.

But Coach Hyatt wasn't listening. She picked up a clipboard and paced back and forth across the locker room. I could tell she was going to give us a pep talk. Coaches always pace back and forth and give you a pep talk when your team is losing. It's the first rule of being a coach.

"I want to ask you ragamuffins a question," Coach Hyatt said. "What's a ten-letter word that means 'first president'?"

"Washington!" we all shouted.

"Right!"

The coach wrote something on her clipboard.

"What does that have to do with football?" I asked.

"Nothing," the coach replied. "I'm working on a crossword puzzle."

She started pacing back and forth again.

"How many states are there?" she asked.

"Fifty!" we all shouted.

"Right! And how many cents are in two quarters?" asked Coach Hyatt.

"Fifty!" we all shouted.

"Right! And what's half of a hundred?" asked Coach Hyatt.

"Fifty!" we all shouted.

"What does that have to do with football?" I asked.

"Nothing," she said. "Fifty is my favorite

number. The point is, this game is half over. That's fifty percent. So we've got fifty percent left. The Sharks had their half. Now it's time for *our* half."

"But we're getting *killed* out there, Coach!" Michael said.

"Don't worry," Coach Hyatt told us. "I have a plan."

A plan? What plan could she possibly have? We were behind by seventy-seven points!

"It's time to bring out our secret weapon," Coach Hyatt said.

She went over to the locker room door.

She put her hand on the doorknob.

And you'll never believe in a million

hundred years who walked into the door at that moment.

Nobody, because if you walked into a door it would hurt. But you'll never believe who walked into the door*way*.

I'm not gonna tell you.

Okay, okay, I'll tell you. But you have to read the next chapter. So nah-nah-nah boo-boo on you.

Our Secret Weapon

It was Andrea Young!!!

Little Miss Perfect I-Know-Everything-and-You-Don't walked into our locker room. And she was wearing a football uniform!

"There's a girl in the locker room!" shouted Neil the nude kid. "Run for your lives!"

"Coach Hyatt is a girl, too, dumbhead," I told Neil.

"Oh, right."

"Hi, Arlo!" Andrea said.

"What are *you* doing here?" I asked her.

"Coach Hyatt asked me to join the team because you boys are so lame," she told me. "I wasn't allowed to wear my jewelry, so I accessorized my helmet with stickers. Do you like it?"

"No," I told her, "and girls don't play football."

"I've been watching Andrea on the sideline," Coach Hyatt told us. "I think she can help us. She's fast. She's strong. She's smart."

"She's annoying," I added.

"Do you want to win, A.J.?" Coach Hyatt asked. "Or do you just want to complain?"

"Can I do both?" I asked.

Coach Hyatt paced the locker room again.

"Do you ragamuffins know what I used to have when I was your age?" asked the coach.

"A log cabin?" I guessed.

"No, a hamster," Coach Hyatt said. "His name was Chip. I loved that hamster. And one day Chip got run over by a bulldozer. Poor little fella. He didn't have a chance. Chip was flattened; and after the bull-dozer ran over him, he was about the size of a living-room rug."

Everybody started sniffling because we were imagining in our heads a hamster getting run over by a bulldozer.

"When you kids go out on the field for the second half," the coach continued, "don't think about winning this game for me. Don't think about winning this game for your parents. Think about Chip, that poor little hamster. Let's go out there and win this one . . . for the Chipper!"

I wasn't sure why we should play any better just because Coach Hyatt's hamster got run over by a bulldozer. But it almost didn't matter what she said, because we all started jumping up and down and chanting *"Chipper! Chipper! Chipper!"* as we ran out of the locker room to start the second half of the game.

The Moose
Goes Nuts

We ran out onto the field and got ready to receive the kickoff. One of the Sharks walked by me.

"You guys are toast." He sneered.

That guy totally made no sense at all. Toast is bread that was in a toaster. I'm a person, and I've never been in a toaster.

How could a person fit inside a toaster, anyway? He'd have to be really small. I'd rather be one of those muffins made of rags.

We lined up, and the Sharks kicked off to start the second half. Andrea picked up the bouncing ball.

She faked left, and some Shark went flying by her.

She faked right, and another Shark missed the tackle.

Andrea was faking left and right, and the Sharks were falling all over themselves trying to tackle her! Everybody started screaming with excitement.

Andrea was running downfield, dancing and leaping past the Sharks. She pirouetted and Irish stepped and hip-hopped around the Sharks. They couldn't lay a hand on her! Finally, Andrea clog danced into the end zone.

Touchdown!

We actually scored! Everybody was going crazy. Football is a lot like dancing, I guess, except that you get to knock guys on their butts.

Suddenly, I didn't feel tired or sore anymore.

Andrea is a really good soccer player, so Coach Hyatt said she could kick the extra point.

Sharks 77, Moose 7.

After we all calmed down, Andrea kicked off. We ran down the field and gang tackled the Shark with the ball. He fumbled it. Andrea scooped the ball up and ran it all the way into the end zone!

Sharks 77, Moose 14.

Coach Hyatt called time-out and gathered us all around her.

"Okay, A.J.," she said, "from now on, I

want you to be our wide receiver."

"But I'm the quarterback!" I protested. "That's my position."

"We're going to try something new," the coach told me. "From now on, Andrea is the quarterback."

"WHAT?! That's not fair!"

"Do you want to win?" Coach Hyatt asked me. "Or do you want to complain?"

"Can't I do both?"

"We're a team!" Coach Hyatt barked. "You ragamuffins picked up my car as a team, and you play as a team! Now go out there and win this one for the Chipper!"

"Who's the Chipper again?" I asked. I had forgotten who the Chipper was.

"My hamster!" Coach Hyatt barked. "He got run over by a bulldozer, remember?"

"Oh, yeah."

I didn't feel good about being replaced as quarterback, but I ran out on to the field anyway.

84

Well, I'm glad I did. Because after that, the Moose just went nuts! With Andrea at quarterback and me at wide receiver, we were unstoppable. Every pass she threw went right into my hands. When the Sharks had the ball, Andrea would intercept their passes and run the ball all the way down the field to score.

We made touchdown after touchdown. Field goal after field goal. Andrea was leaping and diving and spinning and clogging and hip-hopping. The Sharks were totally dazed and confused. It was amazing! Everybody in the bleachers was going crazy.

Sharks 77, Moose 44.

Sharks 77, Moose 51.

Sharks 77, Moose 58.

Sharks 77, Moose 65.

Sharks 77, Moose 72.

After Andrea scored that last touch-down, one of the Sharks went over to her and said, "Hey, kid! Where'd you learn

how to play like that?"

"At the Ballet des Jeunes School of Dance," Andrea replied.

Thanks to Andrea, in the second half we were totally kicking the Sharks' butts! The only problem was that we were running out of time.

The score was 77–72. We were still behind by five points. Coach Hyatt blew her whistle and called time-out to stop the clock.

I looked up at the scoreboard. There were eleven seconds left in the game.

The Secret Play

We all ran to the sideline and huddled around Coach Hyatt.

"Take a knee, kids," she said.

"Where should we take it?" I asked.

"Quiet!" barked Coach Hyatt. Then she started whispering. "Okay, this is it. It's time."

"Time for what?" Ryan asked.

"It's time for The Secret Play," Coach Hyatt told us.

"Oh no!" said Neil the nude kid. "Not The Secret Play! The last time we tried The Secret Play, we fell all over ourselves."

"Yeah," I said. "I almost broke my leg."

"It's going to be different this time," the coach told us. "Now we've got Andrea. You ragamuffins can do this. Just like you picked up my car. Do it for the Chipper."

"Who's the Chipper again?" I asked.

"My hamster!" Coach Hyatt barked.

"Oh, yeah."

The ball was on our twenty-yard line. We had to drive eighty yards in eleven seconds. It looked impossible. We got into position.

"Hut-one!" Andrea shouted. "Hut-two! HIKE!"

Wyatt hiked the ball to Andrea.

Andrea flipped it to Ryan.

Ryan passed it to me at the thirty-yard line.

I shoveled it over to Michael.

Michael ran to the fifty-yard line and lateraled it to Neil.

Neil ran all the way to the ten-yard line and handed it off to Wyatt.

Wyatt ran almost to the goal line, and then he suddenly stopped.

"Run, Wyatt! Run!" we all screamed.

There was no time left on the clock. Wyatt was just standing at the one-yard line. If he didn't score, the game would be over and we would lose.

"RUN!" we all screamed.

A Shark was about to tackle Wyatt!

That's when the weirdest thing in the history of the world happened.

Wyatt picked his nose.

Well, that's not the weird part, because Wyatt picks his nose all the time. The weird part was that Wyatt picked his nose, and then he stuck the booger right on the Shark's face!

Ew, disgusting!

The Shark shoved Wyatt away from him!

Wyatt fell on his butt and landed . . . in the end zone!

Touchdown!

78–77. The Moose win!

Everybody went crazy! You should have been there! Our whole team ran to do the end zone dance. We shook our butts, lifted one of our legs over our heads, hopped up and down for a while, and then put our hands in the air and waved them around like crazy people. Nah-nah-nah boo-boo on the Sharks!

We ran to the sideline, and all the parents were taking pictures of us. It was a real Kodak moment.

"You made a home run!" my mom yelled. I slapped my forehead.

Everybody was going nuts and hugging each other. Andrea came over to me. She opened her arms.

"Give me a hug, Arlo," Andrea said.

"Not gonna happen."

"I want a hug, Arlo," Andrea said.

"Not for a million hundred dollars."

"Come on, Arlo," Andrea said.

"I would rather eat a live-bug sandwich."

We went back and forth like that for a while.

"Arlo, I'm on your *team*!" Andrea said. "Humphf!"

Hmm. Andrea had a point. After a big win like this, you should hug your teammates. Andrea was on our team, and she won the game for us.

But she was a *girl*! If I hugged Andrea, the guys were sure to make fun of me.

I was faced with the hardest decision of my life. I didn't know what to say. I didn't know what to do. I had to think fast. I was concentrating so hard that my brain hurt.

Suddenly, Andrea reached out to grab me.

I faked left.

Then I faked right.

Then I faked left again.

But Andrea didn't fall for my fakes. She wrapped her arms around me and hugged me.

Ugh, disgusting!

"Oooooh!" Ryan said. "A.J. and Andrea are hugging. They must be in *love*!"

"When are you gonna get married?" asked Michael.

Coach Hyatt told everybody to line up. At the end of each game, we have to line up, shake hands with the other team, and say "good game." Nobody knows why.

I shook hands with all the Sharks. When I got to the last one, he grabbed my hand and started squeezing.

"Good game," he told me as he crushed the bones in my hand. "If it weren't for that girl, we would have destroyed you."

I thought I was gonna die.

13

UFM*

On TV, the winning football team dumps Gatorade over the coach's head at the end of the game.

"Hey," I whispered to the guys, "let's dump the Gatorade over Coach Hyatt's head!"

---

* Unidentified Flying Moose

"Great idea, A.J.!" Ryan said.

I should get the No Bell Prize. That's a prize they give out to people who don't have bells.

Coach Hyatt was facing away from us, talking to some parent.

Neil unscrewed the top from the jug of Gatorade. Me and Michael and Ryan grabbed the jug. Wyatt just picked his nose.

"Man, this jug is heavy!" Michael said, grunting.

"Hey, we picked up a car, didn't we?" Ryan said.

We lifted the giant jug and carried it over to Coach Hyatt. The parent she had been talking to was walking away. Coach Hyatt was about to blow her whistle.

That's when we dumped the entire jug of Gatorade over her head.

It was great! Gatorade was everywhere! Coach Hyatt was soaked!

That's when the strangest thing in the history of the world happened.

Coach Hyatt grabbed her throat. It looked like she was trying to say something, but she couldn't. All that came out of her mouth was a whistling noise.

"She's choking!" Ryan yelled. "Her whistle is caught in her throat!"

Coach Hyatt was gagging and looking really scared.

"She can't breathe!" Neil yelled.

"We've got to *do* something!" shouted Emily.

"This is all your fault, Arlo!" Andrea said. "It was *your* idea to dump the Gatorade on her head!"

I looked at Ryan. Ryan looked at Neil. Neil looked at Andrea. Andrea looked at Emily. Everybody was looking at everybody else.

"Does anybody know the Heimlich maneuver?" one of the parents shouted.

The Heimlich maneuver is this thing you do when somebody has something caught in their throat.

"A.J. does!" Ryan yelled.

"That's right!" shouted Andrea. "He

saved my life once."

It was true. One time, Andrea was choking on an apple, and I punched her in the
stomach to make the apple pop out.

I grabbed Coach Hyatt from behind
and punched both of my fists against her

stomach.

The whistle shot out of her mouth.

"You saved my life, A.J.!" said Coach Hyatt.

The whistle kept flying up in the air. And you'll never believe in a million hundred years what it hit.

Rufus the Doofus!

That whistle must have had a sharp edge, because it tore a hole in Rufus.

Rufus started flying crazily around in the air!

Rufus faked left!

Rufus faked right!

Then Rufus must have run out of air, because he was falling out of the sky!

"Run for your lives!" shouted Neil. "It's an Unidentified Flying Moose!"

Everybody freaked out and went running in all different directions and crashing into each other.

Rufus was heading straight for the group of cheerleaders!

And then . . . *WHAM*!

Rufus landed right on Emily!

Emily was on the ground under Rufus, freaking out, like always. It was hilarious.

We saw it live and in person.

"Owwww, my leg!" Emily yelled.

We all gathered around and picked Rufus up off Emily. It was easy, because we had already picked up a Mini Cooper and a jug of Gatorade.

"Are you okay, Emily?" asked Andrea.

"No, I'm not okay!" Emily yelled with tears in her eyes.

Sheesh, what a crybaby! So a moose fell out of the sky and landed on her head. What's the big deal? Stuff like that happens all the time.

"Walk it off," Coach Hyatt told Emily.

"I think it might be broken!" Emily whined.

"Broken?" Coach Hyatt said. "If a moose fell on me when I was your age, I would get up and build a log cabin with my bare hands."

Well, that's pretty much the way it happened. With Andrea on our team, maybe we'll actually win a few games this season. Maybe Emily's leg will heal. Maybe Wyatt the Nose Picker will run out of boogers. Maybe we'll get to ram the Elvis dummy some more. Maybe another moose will fall on Emily's head. Maybe Coach Hyatt will stop building log cabins and get a new hamster. Maybe we'll find out what "ragamuffin" means. Maybe Rent-A-Blimp will be able to patch the hole in Rufus the Doofus.

But it won't be easy!